For Rosemary - Best Wishes

Victoria Chess

June 1986

A Little Touch of
MONSTER

by Emily Lampert

Illustrated by Victoria Chess

The Atlantic Monthly Press
BOSTON   NEW YORK

For Katie, Jamie, and Christopher,
who (I have it on the very best authority)
are always *listened to*

E.L.

For Jasper

V.C.

First edition

Library of Congress Cataloging-in-Publication Data

Lampert, Emily.
    A little touch of monster.

    Summary: Tired of never having his wishes considered,
Parker decides to teach his family a lesson.
    [1. Behavior–Fiction.   2. Family life–Fiction]
I. Chess, Victoria, ill.   II. Title.
PZ7.L1844Li   1985   [E]   85-26847
ISBN 0-87113-022-X

DNP

Published simultaneously in Canada

Printed in Japan

Parker was not a monster.

He did not hide strange things in his sisters' beds, or alarm guests by leaping unannounced from the linen closet.

He did not balance oatmeal on his head at breakfast, or sit on the buttered toast.

He did not drop surprises into the goldfish bowl at Aunt Lydia's, or do unspeakable things to her poodle.

"Isn't he just *scrumptious?*" asked passersby in the park at the very sight of him.

"What a little dumpling!" sighed the salesladies when Parker's mother took him shopping.

"Cute little tyke!" mumbled gentlemen on street corners as they waited for the lights to change.

Cute and dumpled and scrumptious as Parker was, he was almost always noticed. But what Parker *really* wanted was to be listened to.

And he never was.

When Parker's sisters played house and Parker most
definitely did *not* want to be the baby in the bonnet, his
sisters paid no attention.

"Baby's bonnet is too loose!" they would cry, tying
it tighter.

When company came to visit and Parker tried to make
them realize that being bounced on a knee and tossed
in the air interfered with lunch, no one paid any attention.

"Aren't we having a lovely time!" they boomed mer-
rily while Parker was in midair.

When Parker was being fitted for a red velvet suit and the salesladies were firmly buttoning him in, no one paid the slightest bit of attention when Parker said that he preferred blue.

"See how the red matches his dear little cheeks!" gurgled the ladies.

Suddenly one morning Parker did not feel cute. He did not feel like a dumpling. He most definitely did not feel scrumptious. Parker felt like a monster.

"Aarrgh!" growled Parker to his oatmeal at breakfast.

"Uurrgh!" he snarled at the toast, throwing it high in the air.

He crawled under the table and made large menacing
noises at everyone's feet.

"Whatever has come over Parker?" wailed his mother
anxiously, rushing off for a thermometer and aspirin.

But Parker did not say.

Parker did not have a fever so his mother took him
to the park as usual.

"And how *is* this darling child?" gushed the ladies.

"Graaghh!" he yowled. "Yuurrgh!" he added at the
top of his lungs.

"*Ah!*" squeaked the ladies, all aghast.

"Whatever *has* come over Parker?" moaned Parker's mother to herself, shaking her head like a rattle. But Parker did not say.

Parker's mother decided it would be better not to go shopping after all.

She hurried home with Parker to think about it over lunch.

After lunch, Parker's sisters decided to play house.

"Parker," announced the eldest generously, "you can be the baby!" She began to tie the bonnet on him.

"Naahhh!" roared Parker. "WOnonoo!" he bellowed, in case they hadn't heard. "Grubbishh," he mumbled to the rug.

"No?" gasped one sister.

"No!" agreed the other.

"Oh, Parker!" wailed his mother, wringing her hands. "What*ever* has come over you?" And she sent the maid to get an ice bag for her head.

But Parker merely sat grumpily in the middle of the floor. Occasionally he gave a small growl.

It was clear that Parker was not himself.

"What shall we do?" worried Parker's mother from beneath her ice bag.

"What shall we do?" echoed Parker's father from the drawing room. He came and stood in the doorway.

"I think," he declared, "that Parker has a touch of monster coming on."

No one could argue with that.

"People used to pay a great deal of attention to monsters, but now we just pretend they don't exist."

The family looked expectant. Even Parker cocked an ear.

"So!" said Parker's father. "It's obvious we must pay more attention to Parker!"

This seemed quite a sensible idea, although one of Parker's sisters grumbled that they'd been heeding the little monster all day as it was.

"We will start tomorrow," advised Parker's father.

The next morning, everyone got up on tiptoe.

"Parker, dear," whispered his mother attentively at breakfast, "how do you feel about oatmeal and toast today?"

Parker looked up. First he glanced to the right, then to the left.

They all held their breath.

"Egg, please," he said.

Everyone sighed in relief and Parker's mother reached for the bowl of boiled eggs.

"*Not* boiled," continued Parker. "Sunny-side up, cut off the white. And make the toast look like a hat."

Parker's mother was so pleased that Parker seemed to be behaving himself that she didn't mind making a separate breakfast.

"So far, so good, dear," she whispered to Parker's father.

"So far, so good!" thought Parker.

Later that morning, Parker's parents took him shopping. They looked at sweaters.

"Which color do *you* prefer, Parker, dear?" asked his mother.

"Blue is my favorite color!" answered Parker.

The salesladies started to wrap up a blue sweater.

"Not *that* blue," interrupted Parker. "Peacock blue, with green stripes in it."

"Oh," said the salesladies.

"Oh," said Parker's mother.

"Perhaps it can be ordered," said one of the salesladies doubtfully.

Parker's mother looked at Parker's father.

"So far, so good, dear?" she asked.

"So far, so good!" thought Parker.

That afternoon, Parker's sisters wanted to play house.

"Parker," they asked carefully, "who would *you* like to be?"

"The father," announced Parker.

His sisters smiled and started to put the bonnet on a doll.

"No wives or babies!" added Parker. "They are away at sea. You must be the dogs," he decided, and went to wait for his slippers in the drawing room.

His sisters looked at each other.

"So far, so good," they sighed reluctantly.

"So far, perfect!" thought Parker.

The next morning Parker's mother asked Parker how he would like his egg.

"From a crocodile," demanded Parker, "lightly turned over and sprinkled with pink sugar."

"Oh!" said Parker's mother.

"Ugh!" said Parker's sisters.

"Hmmm!" said Parker's father.

"Perhaps tomorrow, dear?" said Parker's mother anxiously. "We're fresh out."

Parker scowled slightly at his boiled egg.

"You can choose what you'd like for lunch and dinner, dear!" offered his mother hastily.

Parker's face brightened. A little touch of monster certainly went a long way!

"Chocolate," he said firmly. "I'll eat nothing but chocolate!"

"Hmmm," said Parker's father thoughtfully.

After breakfast Parker's mother and father went out
to shop. They were gone a long time. When they returned
they disappeared for still longer into the kitchen.

"Lunch is served!" called Parker's mother at last.

Parker looked at his plate. It was heaped with chocolate! Chocolate chicken legs and chocolate carrot sticks.
A tall glass of chocolate milk. And on his bread-and-
butter plate, chocolate bread and chocolate butter.

"Be sure and clean your plates!" admonished Parker's father.

Parker did not need to be asked twice. He gobbled down his chocolate chicken legs. He munched on his chocolate carrot sticks between sips of chocolate milk and tiny bites of chocolate bread and butter.

Finally, Parker's plate was perfectly clean.

"And now for dessert!" said Parker's mother. "Parker's favorite!

"Chocolate ice cream with fudge sauce!" she finished triumphantly.

After lunch Parker was very quiet. At teatime, when his mother produced a chocolate scone especially for him, he said his sisters might prefer it.

When it was time for dinner, Parker's mother had to call him twice to come to the table. Slowly Parker crept to his chair. Slowly he climbed up. He peered over the edge of the table.

"Look, Parker!" said his mother. Parker looked.

Parker gulped.

"Why Parker, dear," his mother asked, "aren't you hungry?"

Parker looked across the table at his mother. He looked at his father. He looked at his sisters.

They looked back.

"You know," said Parker slowly, "monsters love chocolate! They eat it all the time." He pushed at his plate a little. "Maybe we should save this for the next time we have a little monster?" He looked up hopefully.

Parker's father looked thoughtful. His mother dimpled in that certain way she had. His sisters grinned.

"What a fine idea!" they all said; and Parker helped his mother take the chocolate and put it away.

From that day on they did their best to pay attention
to Parker, within reason. In return, Parker did his best
to be well behaved, within reason. In fact, Parker tried
very hard never to be a monster again.